Waddle of
the Penguins

Owlkids Books

Chirp, Tweet, and Squawk loved to play in their playhouse. On this particular day, they were playing…

"Penguins!" said Squawk.

"Penguins waddling in the Antarctic!" added Tweet.

"Penguins waddling in the Antarctic on their way to the South Pole!" shouted Chirp.

"Um, where's the South Pole?" asked Penguin Squawk.

"It's over there!" replied Penguin Tweet.

"Way over there!" said Penguin Chirp.

"It's going to take forever to waddle all the way to the South Pole!" said Squawk.

"Well, penguins don't just waddle," said Chirp. "They also slide!"

"Yahoo! Race you guys!" said Tweet, as she belly flopped onto the snow and slid down a hill.

WHUMP!

"I'm winning!" yelled Squawk, just before he slammed into a snowbank.

"That's got to hurt," said Tweet.

"Why don't we fly?" asked Chirp.

"Penguins can't fly," said Tweet. "But they're really good swimmers."

"Brrr! The water looks super cold," said Chirp.

"Don't worry! Penguins have an extra layer of fat to keep them warm," said Tweet.

"Fat and flippers, don't fail me now!" said Squawk, as he dove into the icy waters.

Penguins Chirp, Tweet, and Squawk flapped their flippers as they flitted and floated in the water.

"Look at me go!" said Squawk.

FLAP! FLAP! FLAP!

Suddenly, a big spout of mist shot up into the sky.

"What is that?" asked Squawk.

"It looks like a water spout!" replied Tweet.

"And where there's a spout…" said Chirp, "there must be a whale!"

"It's a...killer whale!" yelled Chirp.

"Why'd you make it a killer whale?" asked Squawk. "Why not a happy whale?"

"That looks like a *hungry* whale!" said Tweet. "Quick! Swim to that ice floe!"

"Good thing whales can't climb," said Squawk.

"We can't climb, either," said Chirp. "It's too slippery!"

"We're whale food!" shouted Squawk.

"Hurry!" said Tweet. "Look in the, um…cooler for something to help us."

"Cooler?" asked Squawk. "I'm confused. Is it snack time for us or for the whale?"

"She means the box where we keep all the helpful stuff," said Chirp.

"Yeah, by the front door! Let's look inside," said Tweet.

The three friends opened the lid.

"Any whale repellent?" asked Squawk.

"Nope," said Tweet. "But there's modeling clay, a rubber band, a fan, some toothpicks…"

"Toothpicks! Those just might work!" said Chirp.

"What are toothpicks again?" asked Squawk.

"Toothpicks are for picking food out of your teeth," said Chirp. "You can also use their pointy ends to serve food, like fruit and cheese."

"All this talk of food makes me want a snack," said Squawk.

"First, we have to stop the whale from making us *its* snack!" said Chirp.

"But how?" asked Squawk. "By serving it fruit on a toothpick?"

"No, Squawk," said Tweet. "By using the toothpicks to climb the ice!"

Penguins Chirp, Tweet, and Squawk climbed to safety.

But they weren't safe for long!

"Whoa! The whale is trying to knock us off the ice!" yelled Chirp.

"I guess it's still hungry!" said Squawk.

"It's too slippery to hold on!" shouted Tweet, as they slid off the ice...and into the whale's wide-open mouth!

"Whew!" said Chirp. "The good news is the whale didn't swallow us."

"The bad news is we're stuck in its teeth," said Tweet.

"The other bad news is it smells like stinky fish in here!" said Squawk.

"But there's also more good news," said Chirp. "We have toothpicks! So we can pick ourselves out of the whale's teeth!"

Penguins Chirp, Tweet, and Squawk pried themselves loose and then dropped down onto the whale's tongue.

"That was gross!" said Squawk. "But also kind of cool."

"Now what?" asked Chirp.

"I know!" said Tweet. "Whales spout air through their blowholes. If we stand in the right place, the air will push us out when the whale spouts!"

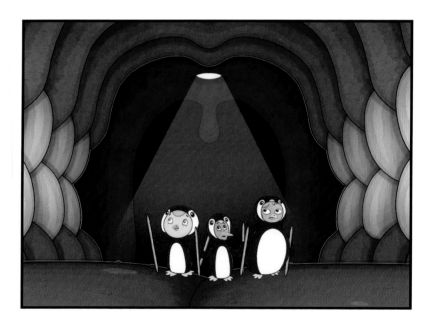

Soon, penguins Chirp, Tweet, and Squawk shot out of the whale's blowhole.

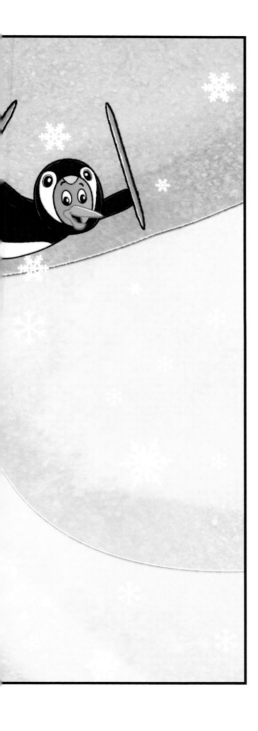

"And you said penguins couldn't fly, Tweet!" said Chirp.

"We're flying on whale-spout power!" said Tweet.

"I'm so hungry, I could eat a whale!" said Squawk, as they soared toward the South Pole.

"We made it!" said Tweet. "This was a *cool* adventure!"

From an episode of the animated TV series *Chirp*, produced by Sinking Ship (Chirp) Productions. Based on the Chirp character created by Bob Kain.

Based on the TV episode *Waddle of the Penguins* written by Diana Moore. Story adaptation written by J. Torres.

Owlkids Books acknowledges the financial support of the Canada Council for the Arts, the Ontario Arts Council, the Government of Canada through the Canada Book Fund (CBF) and the Government of Ontario through the Ontario Media Development Corporation's Book Initiative for our publishing activities.

Published in Canada by
Owlkids Books Inc.
10 Lower Spadina Avenue
Toronto, ON M5V 2Z2

Library and Archives Canada Cataloguing in Publication

Torres, J., 1969-, author
    Waddle of the penguins / adapted by J. Torres.

(Chirp ; 5) Based on the TV program Chirp; writer of the episode Diana Moore.

ISBN 978-1-77147-177-0 (pbk.).--ISBN 978-1-77147-178-7 (bound)

    I. Moore, Diana, 1981-, author   II. Title.

PS8589.O6755667W44 2015   jC813'.54   C2015-903657-7

Edited by: Jennifer Stokes
Designed by: Susan Sinclair

Funded by the Government of Canada
Financé par le gouvernement du Canada

Manufactured in Altona, MB, Canada, in July 2015, by Friesens Corporation
Job #213921

A   B   C   D   E   F

Publisher of Chirp, chickaDEE and OWL
www.owlkidsbooks.com

Owlkids Books is a division of Bayard CANADA